Dear Tuth Ferry,

   My mom is really bizzy so this is the first letter I wrote by myself. I never met a tuth ferry before. What do you look like?

   This is my first lost tuth and I don't know the rules. Toby says if I get money then you get to keep my tuth. Maybe not. Please, my tuth is very speshul to me. Can I keep it? And have the money, too? I would a presheate it.

   Maybe this letter needs a stamp. Maybe not. I'll ask Mom after she gets off the phone. Or Penelope after she stops fighting with Toby about the phone.

                    Your friend,
                    Alex Vandershoot

P.S. Maybe you could do something about my dad's job. If your not too bizzy.

The *T. F.* Letters

by *Karen Ray*

SCHOLASTIC INC.

New York Toronto London Auckland Sydney
Mexico City New Delhi Hong Kong

ISBN 0-439-21783-0

12 11 10 9 8 7 6 5 4 3 2 1   0 1 2 3 4 5/0

Printed in the U.S.A.   40

First Scholastic printing, October 2000

For Alicia, Sabrina, Danny, and David,
siblings without equal.

Chapter 1

When it finally, finally, *finally* happened, Alex Vandershoot was sitting under the kitchen table in a playhouse she had made herself out of sheets and clothespins.

She had arranged her favorite stuffed animals—Alberta, Tiny, and Dingbat—against the opposite table leg and was trying very hard not to think about what it would be like to move a thousand miles away.

Lots of kids she knew couldn't even count to a thousand, but Alex could. It took a long time.

"Alberta, Tiny," she said, "would you care for some brownie?"

She waited long enough for them to answer.

"No?" said Alex. "Wonderful. All the more for Dingbat and me." She swooped up Dingbat and placed the fuzzy batlike creature on her lap.

"Dingbat, you don't care for any either? I *am* surprised at you, Dingbat, turning down Mom's brownies. How many stuffed animals these days get offered fresh made-from-scrap brownies? That's all right. I still love you, Dingbat."

Alex liked to say "Dingbat" as often as possible.

She tried not to listen to her big sister, Penelope, who was sitting at the breakfast bar slurping up brownies and talking on the phone. Penelope thought she was hot stuff because she went to middle school and had her very own tube of Moonlight Santa lipstick.

And Alex especially tried not to listen to her brother, Toby, who was on the couch practicing his trumpet. And probably eating brownies at the same time. Maybe it would help his playing. His spit valve was awful enough without little bits of brownie smooshed in. Disgusting. Many things about Toby were disgusting.

The sheets that made up her playhouse were pink and kept out enough light so you hardly noticed all the dirt on the floor, unless you folded your legs and your anklebone ground into a piece of petrified cheese.

"So, Dingbat, would you like to just sit here while I eat my brown—

"Tiny! Alberta! No bickering." Alex used her father's voice. "You can sit here, too, if you like, with me and Dingbat."

She gathered Alberta, a zebra, and Tiny, an elephant, onto her lap along with Dingbat.

At least *they* would be going along with her.

Alex took a bite of brownie. It was slightly warm and crumbly. Her favorite.

Alex knew Mom was trying to make it up to them.

She wiped her hand on her sweatpants and counted each chew.

One . . .
Two . . .
Three . . .
Four . . .
Five . . .
Six . . .
How long did it take to count to a thousand?
Seven . . .
Eight . . .
Nine . . .
Ten . . .
Eleven . . .
Alex realized with dismay that the brownie was dissolving in her mouth.

A thousand miles away! She'd never get to see Allison or Megan or Jana or her teacher, Mrs. Newsome, again, no matter what her parents said.

She chewed hard.
Twelve . . .
Thirteen . . .
Fourteen . . .
As long as she kept counting she wouldn't be

able to cry. And if she both counted and chewed really hard there wouldn't be room in her mind for those thoughts about never seeing her friends again. Alex chomped. She *would* make it to a thousand.

Fifteen . . .

Sixteen . . .

She hugged Dingbat and tried to ignore Toby's screeching.

Seventeen . . .

Eighteen . . .

Ouch!

The nut messed up her counting, so she swallowed the soupy mush in her mouth and jumped up, thwacking her head on the underside of the table.

"Ouch! Mom!" she called. "Why'd you put nuts in the—"

Alex started to cry. She felt her head for blood. There wasn't any, but her mouth sure tasted funny.

Still crying, Alex removed the nut from her mouth. It was a tooth. Finally, finally!

She was surprised by the jagged parts on the

5

bottom, amazed at how white it was, how shiny, how small.

"Mom! Penelope! Toby!" Alex crawled out from under the table, stabbing her knee on an old Cheerio. "Look, everybody."

Toby's trumpet made it hard to hear anything.

Penelope glanced up from the telephone. "Alex, are you laughing or crying?"

"Both, I guess." She held up the tooth. "Look."

The trumpet stopped. "Oh, neato, blood."

Blood? Alex felt her head again and then realized Toby must be talking about blood from her tooth, or where her tooth used to be. But just as Alex started to investigate, to think about the funny taste in her mouth, to wonder what it would be like to bleed to death, Toby jumped in.

"Mom!" *Ta-daaa,* he tooted his trumpet just in case she hadn't heard. "Mom, Alex lost a tooth!"

How dare he?

Alex charged.

Toby held his trumpet over his head, so she got him full force in the stomach.

6

"That was a rotten thing to do," said Penelope.

"What did I do?" Toby dodged Alex's blows.

"You know what you did," Penelope said.

Alex was too busy hitting to talk.

One . . .

Two . . .

Three . . .

A thousand times, she'd punch him a thousand times.

Four . . .

Five . . .

And then she'd get his trumpet and stomp on that a thousand times.

Six . . .

Seven . . .

Eight . . .

If only it was Toby she was never going to see again!

Nine . . .

"Alex!"

Ten . . .

Eleven . . .

7

"Alex," said Toby, "you better be careful or you're *really* going to lose your tooth."

She opened her hand. It was empty. She squatted down to the floor. There were old Cheerios and bread crumbs and gooey brown stuff and several things that might once have been peas. Nothing white.

Her head hurt. Her knee hurt. Her mouth hurt. A thousand miles.

She felt like one of those cartoons when the tears actually spurt out of a character's eyes.

She scooted around on the floor, looking, but the tears made it hard to see. "Dingbat." She hugged her friend.

"What *is* going on in here?" their mother began.

Toby made a zipping motion across his mouth.

Alex rocked Dingbat.

"Mom," said Penelope quietly, "Alex lost a tooth."

"Alex, that's wonderful news. Now you can be on the tooth chart at school."

No one said anything.

"So, Alex," Mom said brightly, "let's see it. Your *first* tooth."

Alex cried harder.

"She dropped it," said Toby.

"I wonder what the Tooth Fairy will have to say about that?" said Mom.

No one said anything.

"Well," said Mom, "let's all put down our trumpets and help out."

Instantly the four of them were on the floor, scuttling about on hands and knees.

"Good *night* it's filthy down here," Mom said. "Whose job is it to sweep the floor?"

"Don't know, Mom," said Penelope. "We'll have to check the chart."

Alex started to look over at the chart, but that would be hopeless, so she stopped herself. The chart was a complicated schedule of chores posted on the refrigerator. Some jobs changed weekly, some monthly. Some—like cleaning the toilets—rotated among family members. Others—like serving dessert—were drawn by lot, or passed out as a reward.

There were good things about the chart—it was easy to get out of doing things. And there were bad things about the chart—a lot of things didn't get done. Then they blamed the chart. Even Mom. Especially Mom.

Sometimes Alex thought this was weird. Other mothers had schedules of what was for dinner, went to an office to work, wore dresses when they came for cafeteria duty, and forced their kids to do stuff.

Mom, however, planned the dinner menu after they got home from school. She ran her greeting-card business from the kitchen table, wore overalls to the cafeteria, and hated chores as much as the rest of them.

The moving was Mom's fault.

Alex couldn't tell exactly what Dad did. Something to do with money in a big company—one that wasn't going to be so big anymore. Because of that, Dad's job was going away. They didn't know when precisely, but soon, sometime soon.

Until then Dad dragged off to work every day and home in the afternoon, never knowing when "it" would happen. He tried not to be cranky with them. And even when he was sad, he organized family projects for them on the weekends. And he had the best lap, especially when he sat really still with his arms around her.

No, Alex didn't blame Dad.

But Mom . . . she ran things. She knew how much they wanted to stay in Texas. And if Mom really wanted to, she could make them stay here. Alex just knew it.

Dad went to work, but Mom was important, he always said. She'd picked out this house by herself. She bought the furniture. She painted their rooms. She put them to bed at night and got them up in the morning. She was even famous, for gosh sakes. She was on TV one time when some of her cards won a prize.

"Hey, Alex," said Toby, "why don't you look over here?"

Alex tried to stay angry at them. Mom had care-

11

fully shaken out and folded the sheets from the playhouse. Toby and Penelope were looking hard for her tooth. Mom even had the broom out.

"Really, Alex," said Toby, "you need to come look over by me."

She saw Toby and Mom glance at each other.

"Go help your brother," said Mom.

Alex squatted down and started to cry again as she realized she had gotten a smudge of blood on Dingbat's head.

"Over there." Toby pointed in the corner next to the window.

She scooched over so she could bump into Toby accidentally. Brothers could be such brats. "Yeah, yeah." Alex got on all fours like the rest of them.

"I *found* it!" Alex jumped up, holding the tooth tightly in her fist.

"Wonderful!" Toby was being nice all of a sudden. It made Alex suspicious.

They all admired the pearly tooth that sat, gleaming, in her outstretched palm.

The tooth was so white it practically glowed.

Her parents were always talking about how grown-up she was. Here, finally, was the proof, a speck of white that beamed with importance in her hand. But even better was the special secret space in her mouth.

Alex's tongue explored the huge emptiness on her bottom gum. The tooth looked so small. How could there be such a gap? Still, there was so much to think about she couldn't dwell on any one thing too long. Her head still hurt. Already the blood in her mouth was gone. There was a slight puffiness about the gum, a softness she'd never experienced before, and *there*—she kept stuffing her tongue in the spot—was that the new tooth coming in already? She needed to go to the bathroom and check the mirror.

"I'm jealous, Alex," said Penelope. "I'm all done with the Tooth Fairy."

"Yeah," said Toby, "what are you going to do with the money?"

13

Alex shrugged. "I'm still trying to decide what to do with my tooth. I thought maybe it would make a pretty necklace. What do you think, Mom?"

"Don't be stupid," said Toby. "The Tooth Fairy keeps your tooth."

No. Like exactly how big a thousand is, this was something that Alex didn't want to think about.

"Of course, you don't *have* to put the tooth under your pillow," Toby said. "You just won't get any money then."

Alex frowned. She liked having money in her piggy bank. Money meant ice-cream cones and chocolate-chip cookies from Becker's, even if it was the end of the month and Mom was broke.

"Mom? What am I going to do? I've waited forever to lose this tooth and I want to keep it, but . . ."

Mom thought a moment. "Why don't you write the Tooth Fairy a note?"

Alex liked writing letters.

She sat at the kitchen table with her tooth in

14

a cereal bowl and the box of stationery from her grandmother Edith in front of her. The writing paper was very pretty, a light pink color with flowers in the corners. There were lines so her words wouldn't fall down the paper.

Alex chewed her pencil. Actually, what she liked was *receiving* letters.

She'd never written anything like this before. It seemed so selfish. *"Please give me the money and let me keep my tooth."* That was what she wanted to say.

"Mom?" she asked.

"Um?" Mom stirred two pots on the stove, then asked Penelope to name the three states of matter, then got mad at Toby for being on the phone so long.

"Mom, what do you think I should say to the Tooth Fairy?"

Toby hung up the phone.

"That's easy," Penelope said. "Solid, liquid, and gas."

"Good, Penelope."

The phone rang.

"Toby!" Mom pretended to slap his hand. "You may not have a brownie right now."

"Okay. Phone's for you."

Alex went back to her pencil.

She wrote very slowly and carefully, without stopping.

> Dear Tuth Ferry,
>
> My mom is really bizzy so this is the first letter I wrote by myself. I never met a tuth ferry before. What do you look like?
>
> This is my first lost tuth and I don't know the rules. Toby says if I get money then you get to keep my tuth. Maybe not. Please, my tuth is very speshul to me. Can I keep it? And have the money, too? I would a presheate it.
>
> Maybe this letter needs a stamp.

16

Maybe not. I'll ask Mom after she gets off the phone. Or Penelope after she stops fighting with Toby about the phone.

Your friend,

Alex Vandershoot

P.S. Maybe you could do something about my dad's job. If your not too bizzy.

As Alex wrote the last word, she heard the back door.

"Look, Dad! I lost a tooth!"

"Fantastic." He picked her up and twirled her around.

Alex folded the letter carefully and addressed it to "The Tuth Ferry." Toby and Penelope were still fighting. Mom was on the phone again. Dad was changing his clothes. Alex got a stamp, licked it, and stuck it on the letter.

✳

That night, Dad kissed her and did prayer and even gave her a whisker kiss.

"You sure look like a big girl with that tooth missing."

"I've been big a long time. I can count to a thousand. Do you want to hear?"

"Not right now. You have a good sleep."

He snapped off the light. But she couldn't sleep.

Would the Tooth Fairy come at a certain time? Would she make noise? How would she get in the house?

Alex got up and opened the window a crack.

Alex felt under her pillow for the fifth time. The letter was still there. How did the Tooth Fairy know where to come? Did she ever miss someone? Get too busy?

Alex was almost asleep when she heard the door squeak. Her eyes flew open, but just for a moment. It was only Penelope.

When Alex woke up she knew there was something special about this morning. After she yawned,

18

her tongue went right to the open space in the front of her mouth.

Of course!

Alex shoved her hand under the pillow. There was an envelope.

It was addressed: "Alexis Beatrice Vandershoot."

Wow. How did the Tooth Fairy know her middle name?

The envelope was long, pale yellow, and lettered in a fancy way.

Alex held it gently, still hardly believing it could be real. She felt every part of it. On the back, at the

19

point of the flap, was a circle of wax the size of a quarter. Alex knew that before they invented glue, kings used wax on envelopes.

"Wow," she whispered, almost afraid the magical envelope would dissolve in her hand. She felt carefully and could make out, in one corner, the outline of a coin and, in the other, the bump of a tooth. She glanced over to make sure that Penelope was still sleeping.

Very slowly Alex slid her finger under the flap and broke the seal. A bit of wax fell on her pajamas. Carefully Alex picked it up and set it on the nightstand.

She opened the envelope. Sure enough, there was the tooth and there was the quarter. And *there* was a letter.

Alex slid the paper out of the envelope.

Dear Alexis,
As you know, usually it is a swap,
your tooth for money, but in this case I

can make an exception, if you promise to keep and treasure your tooth as much as I would.

What do I look like?

Use your imagination. Sometimes I wear fairy clothes. Sometimes I wear overalls. Always, I care about children like you.

Sorry about your father's job. I am never ever too busy to help out when I can, but jobs really aren't my department.

Keep wiggling those teeth.

Best wishes,
The Tooth Fairy

Chapter 2

It was a few weeks later when Megan leaned toward Alex so she could be heard in the noisy cafeteria. "I'll trade you my peanut-butter-and-raisin sandwich for your sunflower seeds."

"I'll trade you my chocolate-chip cookies *and*"— Jana reached into her pocket—"a nickel for your sunflower seeds."

Alex smiled. It was fun having something everyone else wanted. Sunflower seeds had been Alex's idea. She loved eating them. The salty flavor in your mouth, the little pop when you broke open the shell, and then the little seed inside—the prize. Her mom had bought six big bags from the bargain bin for fifty cents each. No need to mention that. Alex was the first and, so far, only girl to bring sunflower seeds to school. She'd loved showing the other girls how to eat them, and she especially loved the fact that sunflower seeds had been her idea to begin with.

"What about this?" said Allison. "I'll throw away your trash and push you on the swing at recess for your sunflower seeds."

Alex put her finger on her chin and pretended to make up her mind. Under the table, Alex fingered a secret. She wasn't quite ready yet. They were going to be so surprised.

"How gross," said Jana as a banana peel came flying from the boys' table behind them. They all ducked in case more food groups came flying their way.

Alex, Jana, Allison, and Megan always sat next to the wall at the end of the long table. That way they didn't have to worry about being teased by the bratty girls or listen to the Lisa Girls. The center of the Lisa Girls was, of course, Lisa. And her girls were always interested in whatever Lisa was interested in. Usually it was horses, but for a while it was yo-yos and then it was jump rope. There were complicated rules that went along with being a Lisa Girl, and they seemed to change all the time. One week socks with lace, the next week pigtails.

Alex absently wiggled her loose tooth. The whole idea of those rules, of Lisa, made Alex nervous. She was happy to be regular. That's what Jana, Allison, Megan, and Alex called themselves. The Regulars. One day they might play horses, the next day yo-yos, the next day jump rope. They could wear whatever they wanted. They took turns choosing games. And they never got jealous. Almost never.

Megan had moved here from Ireland at the beginning of second grade. She had such a pretty voice. At the beginning of the year Megan had been sort of Special Regular, but now she was just like the rest of them.

Allison, Jana, and Megan still stared at Alex, waiting.

"What about it, Alex?" asked Allison. "I'll throw

away your trash and push you on the swing *for the rest of the week!*"

Megan and Jana frowned at Allison. That was too much, and they all knew it.

Alex hated it when they fought. It was time.

"I've thought over your offers very carefully, and . . ." Alex pulled out a plastic bag and dangled it above the table.

The three girls leaned in, waiting for Alex's decision.

Alex paused. "And you are such good friends that I brought you *all* some sunflower seeds." She passed out three more little bags.

"For free?" asked Jana.

"Of course for free," whispered Megan. "Don't you know a present when you get one?"

"Thanks," cried Jana.

"Yes, thanks," added Allison.

"Thank you," said Megan.

"You're welcome," said Alex, wondering if they noticed that she'd counted the seeds so each bag had exactly the same number. Seventy-five.

Soon there was sucking and popping around the table as the Regulars ate seeds in their own favorite ways.

Alex and Jana were poppers. They sucked the seed long enough to get the taste, but not long enough to get it soggy. Then they'd tip it endwise on the teeth and pop it open.

Megan was a chipmunk, putting a small handful in her mouth and moving them from left to right as she shelled them.

Allison put the seed in her mouth, popped it, then removed the kernel with her fingers instead of her teeth. This meant her mouth was not as occupied as the other girls'.

"Alex, it was so nice of you to give us these," she said as she picked apart a tricky seed. "We're going to miss you when you leave."

"Yeah," said Jana, "do you know yet when it's going to be?"

Alex looked quickly at Megan. She knew what it was like to move a thousand miles away.

Moving day was all Alex could think about. It

was more important than the last day of school. More important even than her birthday.

Jana and Allison stared at her, waiting.

Summer, she thought heavily. That's when they were moving. Summer. She looked away. "Summer" was supposed to be a good word—no school—but to Alex it was a bad word coming too soon.

"My cousins moved once," said Jana. "They even put their car in the truck! Are you going to get a really big truck?"

Alex shrugged.

"Look, guys," said Megan. "I got this seed that's all white. Most of them are striped, but this one's one color."

"Neato," said Allison. "Watch. I've been practicing at home with raisins." Allison tossed a sunflower seed in the air and caught it in her mouth.

Soon there was a pile of empty wet shells on the table. Megan, Allison, and Jana tossed and caught or tried to toss and catch. Several seeds went on the floor. One made it to the boys' table.

Robert tossed the sunflower seed back, aiming for Jana's mouth, but he missed. He broke his bread crust into pieces and threw that. Then Allison, Jana, and Megan aimed sunflower seeds at the boys' mouths.

It looked like fun. Tossing and catching. If this were a normal day, Alex would be playing with them. Instead, she just sat there, thinking, sucking on a sunflower seed. Sucking hard, trying to get the last speck of flavor out of that seed. She sucked hard. She watched and sucked and—

Pop.

And there, in the middle of her tongue, was her tooth. Alex smiled.

"Hey, everybody, look." She shoved her tongue through the double-wide space on her bottom gum and held out the tooth on the palm of her hand. "Better than a white sunflower seed, right?"

"But not so rare," said Allison.

Alex frowned. Allison already had a whole mouthful of huge teeth.

"It's a very pretty tooth," said Megan.

"Come on, guys," said Jana, "our table just got excused." She swiped the pile of shells off the table into her lunch bag.

Alex hardly ever got the itch to clean up. But as she folded up her sweatshirts and tossed things out from under the bed, it gave her time to think.

Afterward she chewed on the pencil and stared at the paper in front of her. If she wrote an especially good letter, and had a clean room, maybe the Tooth Fairy would be more likely to do what she asked.

Dear Tuth Ferry, she wrote.

That was the easy part. Alex chewed on her pencil.

Thank you so much for letting me keep my tuth last month. I promise always to take good care of it. My tuth, and your letter, are in my secret hiding place in my underware drawer. I am

glad to know you care about children like me.

This time I have another favor that may be harder. Maybe not.

I don't want to move. I know you said jobs aren't your department, but Mom says if money grows on trees we can stay. How about that? I know you can do it.

Your friend,
Alexis Beatrice Vandershoot

P.S. How did you know my middle name?

Alex brushed her teeth half an hour early that night, put on her best nightgown, and brushed her hair. Then she opened the window a crack before getting under the covers.

"Mom," she called, "I'm ready!"

"Just a second."

31

It was always more than a second. Alex started counting, medium speed. She was at two hundred forty-seven when the door opened.

"You're ready early this evening." Mom sat on her bed. "And you've been busy. Your half of the room looks wonderful."

"Thank you." Alex smiled.

"What's the special occasion?"

Alex shrugged. Was that a lie? Alex didn't know, but she felt very certain that if she told, the Tooth Fairy wouldn't come. That was the way magic worked.

"You had a big day today, sweetie. Can I see your mouth?"

Alex smiled, extra wide so the big space on the bottom would show.

Mom smiled her best smile. "You look so cute. And you said the top ones are loose, too?"

Alex nodded.

"Pretty soon we're going to have to make porridge for you for dinner."

Alex didn't say anything. Usually she wanted Mom to stay with her as long as possible at bedtime. Not tonight.

"Is there anything you want to talk about this evening?"

"No."

"Okay." Mom set the water glass on the night-stand Alex shared with Penelope. And they said prayer together. And Mom gave her a snuggle-bug kiss, two on the forehead, two on the chin, and one on the nose, followed by a hug.

The window was closed. That was the first thing Alex noticed when she woke up.

Had it been closed the other time?

She couldn't remember.

Alex hugged herself, wanting to delay the won-derful magic of the letter. There would be another letter, she just knew it. The Tooth Fairy wouldn't let her down.

Slowly she inched her hand under the pillow.

There.

She made sure Penelope was gone before snatching out the envelope.

It was cream colored this time, and her name was lettered in gold, sparkling gold. There was even a little gold swirl under her name.

Alexis Beatrice Vandershoot

Alex had never seen anything so fancy. She popped the seal, eager to see how the Tooth Fairy was going to work it out.

There was the quarter, as she expected, and her

34

tooth, but that wasn't what she was looking for.

Dear Alexis,

What a lovely tooth, dear girl. Take good care of it. About the money growing on trees. Quarters, one at a time, are all I can spring for. Please think a minute. Would you ask Santa Claus to come when you lose a tooth? Or expect magic beans from the Easter Bunny?

I care more about you and know more about you than you will ever guess— middle names are easy—but there are strict rules about what we magical creatures can do.

Otherwise, every spelling test would be an A, vegetables would be an endangered species, and there would be ponies in bedrooms all over town.

Best wishes,
The Tooth Fairy

Chapter 3

Dad helped Toby stir the custard. Penelope whipped the egg whites. Alex hugged Dingbat in one arm and a big box of salt in the other.

"Carol," said Dad, "won't you help?"

"Not if we want Carol's Custom Cards to stay in business." Mom sighed at the piles of papers and ribbons in front of her. "And I'm afraid that right now staying in business is a must."

"Are these egg whites stiff enough?" Penelope asked.

Dad lifted out the beaters to check. "A little more. Then you can do the cream."

"Mom," asked Penelope, "can I have Erica over?"

"Sure—"

"Sorry, dear." Dad kissed Penelope quickly on the forehead. "This is quality time."

"Erica's a quality girl."

"*Family* quality time."

"I can think of a lot better quality things than *cooking*," said Toby.

Toby was wrong. Alex loved having them all cheerful, working on a very yummy project. Having even Dad in a good mood. It was the first warm weekend of spring and almost three weeks since she'd lost a tooth. That was how Alex had started to measure time. With her mouth.

"Fine, Toby," Dad said. "You don't have to eat any."

"I'll have his share," said Alex.

"Fat chance." Toby kept stirring.

Dad checked over the ice-cream freezer, wiping out the inside, making sure the crank moved freely. "Don't let me forget the vanilla. It goes in last, after the mixture cools a bit, and I've been known to leave it out."

"Don't forget the vanilla," said Toby.

"Don't forget the vanilla," said Penelope.

"Honey," called Mom, "don't forget the vanilla."

Alex smiled. "Hey, Dad, don't forget the vanilla!"

"You guys are *soooo* funny." Dad set the little bottle of vanilla on the counter.

It had been almost a year—last summer—since they made ice cream. Alex couldn't remember exactly why they needed this big box of salt. But she knew that once they got to the fun part, the cranking, the salt would become very important. Alex hugged the salt and Dingbat and went to see Mom.

Mom sat at the table with a huge stack of cards, a paper punch, and a zillion little strips of ribbon.

Mom was such a good drawer. On the cards Alex saw a family with their little dog. Mom was punching a hole on each side of the dog's neck and tying the ribbon so it looked like the little dog was actually wearing the ribbon.

Alex knew her mother got different kinds of jobs.

Fun jobs—good jobs—put her in a nice mood. Pay-the-rent jobs meant she was only doing it for the money and might not be in a good mood.

"Mom, is this a *good* job?"

"Well . . ." She tied a ribbon around the little dog's neck. "I guess you could call this a pay-the-mortgage job."

Alex frowned. "More gage?"

"It's like rent, only more so."

Only more so. That must mean she was getting paid a lot for these puppy dogs with ribbons. That was good. Especially now. "Can I help?"

"Sure, you can help." Mom reached for a pencil and made little dots on either side of the dog's neck on five different cards. "Punch a hole where I've put each dot."

Punch. Punch. Alex lined up each dot before she punched.

"Good. When you finish those and feel confident about where the holes go, you can start on the big stack."

Punch. Punch. "I feel confident."

Tie. "Good. Be careful because I don't have any extras."

Punch. Punch. Alex slowed down as she started on the cards without dots. One hole belonged just below the droopy ear and the other, above the shoulder, so the ribbon would look like it was around the dog's neck. No extras. Mom really trusted her.

They worked side by side for several minutes. Alex counted how many cards she'd done. Nineteen, so far. The going rate for helping was a penny a card, but Alex decided not to mention that.

"I want everybody to notice," Dad called, "that I am adding the vanilla."

Punch. Punch. Alex glanced nervously toward the kitchen.

"It's all right," said Mom. "You can go."

Alex swooped up the salt and Dingbat.

They made a sort of parade out back, Dad carrying the ice-cream freezer, Toby with the bag of ice, Alex with the salt, and Penelope, last, walking slowly with the big bowl of soupy white stuff that was going to be ice cream.

"I get to turn first," said Toby.

Dad poured the mixture into the inner bucket and inserted the dasher, the long squiggly thing that would stir it as they cranked.

"I get to lick the dasher," said Toby.

"Toby," said Dad, "you get to add the ice."

Toby scooped the ice into the four-inch space between the inner and outer containers.

Alex opened the box of salt.

Toby kept scooping the ice, swatting his hands on his jeans when they got too cold.

Dad nodded at Alex.

Alex poured salt over the ice.

Dad tinkered with the crank to loosen it up. "Remember what the salt is for?"

Alex shook her head.

"The salt makes the ice colder"—he gave a few easy cranks to get it started—"and that helps the ice cream freeze better. Alex, go ahead."

"Dad," Toby complained, "you said I could go first."

"No," Dad said, "*you* said you could go first."

Alex gave Toby a smarty smile.

"It gets harder as it goes along," Dad continued, "so Alex should go first. She can crank until she gets tired."

Alex decided to crank to a thousand. Very fast. *One, two, three*—

"Slow down," said Dad, "or we'll end up with butter instead of ice cream."

Four, five, six . . .

Dad held the freezer steady while she cranked.

Seven, eight, nine . . .

Every time Alex cranked she wiggled her loose tooth with her tongue. Both big ones in front on the top were loose, but the left one especially.

Ten, wiggle, *eleven*, wiggle . . .

If she could just get the left tooth a little looser, she'd really be able to gross out Mom.

Penelope poured on more salt.

"See the frost forming outside the freezer," Dad said. "Salt water freezes at a much lower temperature than plain water. Zero degrees Fahrenheit is the coldest temperature of an ice-and-saltwater mix."

"And a hundred degrees," Toby imitated him, "is the approximate temperature of the human body."

"Guess I told you that before."

"Every time we make ice cream," said Penelope.

Alex didn't remember that, but since she didn't want to lose track—*twenty-three,* wiggle, *twenty-four,* wiggle—she didn't say anything.

"Have I told you that saltwater is poisonous to plants, and that's why—"

"—we keep the freezer on the driveway," finished Penelope, "where the saltwater won't get on the lawn."

Thirty-six, wiggle, *thirty-seven,* wiggle . . .

Alex decided to slow down a little . . . anything to annoy Toby. Too bad she wasn't getting a penny for each crank.

"Okay." Dad laughed. "Since you've already

heard everything I have to say, how about I listen to what you have to say."

Forty, wiggle, *forty-one,* wiggle . . .

No one said anything.

"I mean," said Dad, "about the move."

Still no one said anything. For a long time no one said anything.

"I want my own room," Penelope said.

"I want a tree house," said Toby.

Dad nodded. "We can't promise anything, but we'll try and make this move as pleasant as possible for everyone. What about you, Alex?"

Was she on fifty-two or sixty-two? It was hard to listen and count at the same time.

Alex spoke very fast. "I'm not going to California. I'm going to live with Megan. She said it was okay."

Dad didn't say anything.

Alex shifted so she could crank with two hands. *Sixty-three,* wiggle, *sixty-four,* wiggle, *sixty-five,* wiggle . . .

"Alex is getting tired," said Toby.

"Am not."

Dad put a hand on Alex's shoulder. "Alex can crank as long as she likes."

She stuck out her tongue at Toby.

"I can't *believe* you let her do whatever she wants."

Seventy-two, shove, *seventy-three,* shove . . .

Dad helped brace the freezer as she cranked.

Eighty-one, shove, *eighty-two,* shove . . .

Her tooth was really starting to come loose.

"This move means big changes for everyone, but your mother and I will do our best to make sure that there's good in it for all of us.

"Since we'll be renting a house in a small town we may be able to afford a little more space. Everyone wants different things. Your mother would like a studio. *I*"—he paused meaningfully—"would like a dog."

"Oh, Daddy, that's wonderful." Penelope kissed him, sideways, so she wouldn't mess up her lipstick.

"How about a Saint Bernard?" said Toby.

A hundred-six, shove, *a hundred-seven,* shove . . .

A dog for moving away from their friends? It was like paying them. Couldn't Toby and Penelope see that?

Anger gave energy to Alex's arms. This whole afternoon—making ice cream, "quality time"—was one big bribe.

"I don't know about the Saint Bernard, son." Dad poured in more ice and salt. "We'll have to wait and see. We plan to make the actual move into a family vacation. Maybe stop at the Grand Canyon or the caves in New Mexico."

"Can we go to Hollywood," Penelope asked, "and Disneyland?"

"Yeah," said Toby, "Disneyland."

"We'll all look at the map together and figure out the best route."

"How long will it take to get to California?" asked Toby.

Dad moved a piece of ice that was sticking. "Depends, but about a week if we drive a few hundred miles each day."

That didn't make sense. Alex kept cranking.

47

Seven days in a week. Three hundred miles a day. No sense at all.

"But that's too far," she protested.

"That's how far it is," said Dad. "Dallas to Northern California is about seventeen hundred miles."

"No!" Alex's stomach felt sick. "You said it's one thousand miles!"

"I would never say—"

"You said it, Dad," said Penelope.

"Yeah," said Toby, "you did. The first time we talked about moving."

"I did?" Dad put his hand around Alex's and helped her crank. "Well, what I meant is that we are moving very far away."

"You didn't say 'far away,' you said 'a thousand miles.'"

"I really don't see what difference it makes."

Four things happened at once. Alex started to cry. She pulled her hand out from under Dad's. She hit her head on the crank.

"It makes a big difference!"

It was only as she ran inside that Alex realized the fourth thing. Her front tooth had fallen out.

Dear Tuth Ferry,
    Why do grown-ups think it doesn't matter what they say to kids?
    Remember my friend Megan? She lost a hole bunch of teeth. Her mom makes really good egg plan cassaroll. Maybe I could live with her. Maybe not. What do you think?
        Your friend,
            Alexis Beatrice Vandershoot

P.S. I can count to a thousand. How high can you count?

Alex tucked in Tiny, Alberta, and Dingbat for the fourth time. No, the fifth. Her tossing and turning kept messing them up.

"Penelope," Alex called, "are you awake?"

No answer.

Alex was worried. What if she couldn't go to sleep at all?

Then *she* wouldn't come, that's all there was to it. Alex knew that.

She glanced over at the slightly open window.

Finally Alex got a great idea. She decided to stay very still, with her eyes closed, and *pretend* to be asleep. She would breathe so slowly and lie so still that even Dingbat wouldn't know the difference. And if she happened to catch a glimpse of the Tooth Fairy through her eyelashes, well, no one would have to know.

When the sun hit her eyes, Alex snatched the envelope out from under her pillow, hardly glancing at the pretty painting on the front before she carefully broke the seal.

Dear Alex,
    Of course I remember Megan—pretty red hair, seventeen freckles, very fine

teeth. I understand why you think it might be calmer at her house right now. But if you promise not to tell, I will let you in on a secret. Megan doesn't know that next year she is moving back to Ireland. That is about five thousand miles away.

I am not the best counter in the world. Mostly I don't worry about it, just worry about how I'm going to get to all those children each evening.

Alex, I know you are very worried about this move, but why don't you take a little advice from an old gal who has traveled a great deal and done all manner of unusual things.

Try not to worry so much about the whens, the whys, and the whatsits of the move. There are probably a great many things that even your parents don't know yet. But one day, it will happen and then everything will be fine and you will wonder why you worried so much about it. Someday you may really need those worries, so don't use them all up now.

Goodness gracious, this letter has gotten long. I've got many more teeth to go before I sleep.

Your friend,
The Tooth Fairy

P.S. Grown-ups—especially your parents—care very much what they say to children. But sometimes they get to worrying and thinking about grown-up things and they don't think before they speak. That's wrong, but your parents aren't perfect any more than you are perfect. (I know that when you clean up your half of the room, you just throw everything in the closet.)

Chapter 4

"Open wide," said Mom.

Alex opened.

"Wider."

Alex stretched her jaw muscles. It was nine days since her last tooth day.

Mom squatted down to look inside Alex's mouth. They were already late for car pool. "Maybe the light is better this way." Mom turned Alex toward the window.

Alex shoved her tongue around, feeling the empty spaces in front. It was much easier to see the new tooth in the mirror than it was to feel it with her tongue.

"Alexis, will you *please* hold still."

Alex took a big breath and became a statue.

"Mom," sighed Penelope, "I'm going to be late."

"Just a minute, guys. Alex says her tooth hurts and I'm trying to—"

"I don't *say* it hurts," said Alex. "It really hurts."

"It's okay if we're late." Toby put his backpack down.

"Here, Mom." Penelope handed over a small mirror from her purse.

"Ugh." Alex gagged at the taste of makeup.

"Hold still!"

Alex froze again.

Mom positioned the awful-tasting mirror behind Alex's top teeth.

"Oh my good—" Mom slapped her free hand over her mouth and shoved the mirror back toward Penelope. "Come on, guys, time for school."

Nobody moved.

"What's wrong with my mouth?"

"I'll call the dentist this morning"—Mom picked

up her purse and keys—"and ask her to take a look at it."

"Take a look at *what*?"

"Well . . . there's a black spot on the back of your front tooth."

Alex was careful to keep her mouth closed that morning. It was hard to pay attention during math, but Alex's ears pricked up when Mrs. Newsome started the science lesson.

"Have you ever noticed," asked Mrs. Newsome, "that yucky stuff that grows on old bread?"

She held up a square green something that probably used to be a piece of bread.

"Ugh," said Jana.

"Disgusting," said Robert

"Looks like puke," said Lisa.

"Puke," said the Lisa Girls.

"Yes, class," said Mrs. Newsome, "mold is kind of disgusting. It's also interesting." She wrote MOLD up on the board.

"Mold is caused by something called mold spores, sort of like invisible seeds that float around the air and can start growing on almost any organic surface, particularly one that's unclean or old.

"Mold grows best in warm, damp places, but it can grow anywhere, the desert, or the ice caps . . . or your refrigerator." Mrs. Newsome opened up an ice chest. "In a few minutes you're going to start growing your own mold. But first, let's look at some more examples.

"Mold can grow on cheese." She held up a spotty orange cube.

"Ugh!"

"Mold can grow on fruit." She held up a disgusting peach.

"Gross!"

"Mold can grow on vegetables." She held up a shriveled ear of corn.

"Disgusting!"

"Isn't this fun?" Mrs. Newsome smiled. "When your parents ask what we did today, you can tell them we looked at rotten food!

"That's what mold is, nature's way of breaking down—or rotting—old things. There are many different kinds of molds. Some are harmful to people and some are helpful, very helpful. Some molds are green." She held up the bread. "Some are white." She held up the cheese. "And some are black." She held up the corn.

"One of the most important and useful discoveries in all of science came from mold that is now used in medicines . . ."

Alex put her hands over her mouth. She couldn't listen anymore.

That's what it was. It had to be.

She went over the evidence. *"Mold grows best in warm, damp places. . . . Some molds are harmful to people. . . . Some are black."*

No doubt about it.

The part about rotting and unclean places had her especially worried. You were supposed to brush after every meal, Alex knew, but no one ever did. Even at night before bed there were times she only sort of brushed. Oh, she didn't just wet the toothbrush like Toby, but she didn't brush very well either.

Alex's tooth hurt. And she was hungry. Since it hurt to bite down, even on a banana, she hadn't eaten much the past few days.

And it was all her own fault.

Alex could just imagine the awful mold, covering up her whole tooth. It was probably on the roof of her mouth now—that hurt *a lot*—and then moving to her tongue and . . . she didn't want to think about it, but Alex knew she was rotting. Actually rotting.

Mrs. Newsome kept waving around the gooshy old peach, and all Alex could think about was that the same thing was happening to her insides. She was going to die; that's all there was to it. No need to worry about moving because she was going to die instead.

Alex's stomach hurt even more, and her throat started to close up.

Maybe she was dying right now, rotting before recess.

Her eyes started to water, and she had a terrible time breathing—

"Alex." The teacher was standing at her desk, touching her shoulder. "Your mother is at the office."

Mom kissed Alex on the forehead before she turned the key. "How ya doing, sweetheart?"

"It hurts, Mom."

"I know. Dr. Susan's office was very good about letting us come this morning."

Alex nodded, unsure of how much to say. "Mom, why didn't you believe me that it hurt until you saw the black spot?"

"It's not that I didn't believe you." Mom took Alex's hand. "Maybe I've been thinking too much about grown-up stuff. Or maybe I thought the tooth was getting ready to come out—you've been losing them awfully fast."

"But none of the other teeth hurt before they came out." Alex thought out loud. "I've been telling you for days that it hurts."

59

Mom patted Alex's leg. "We'll find out what it is in just a few minutes."

Alex *knew* what the spot was. She felt the front of her mouth with her tongue. Her tongue wanted to go in the open space on the left, but she aimed it at the big tooth on the right instead.

The tooth moved outward slightly under pressure, but much as she tried Alex couldn't feel the black spot. It was there, though. Mom would never make up anything so terrible.

Alex felt the front of her mouth again. Not with her finger—she wasn't about to get any of those nasty mold sports on her hand—but still with her tongue.

There.

On the gum just behind the sore tooth was a puffy bump. She felt it again. It seemed softer than the other parts of her mouth, but it was hard to tell with her tongue.

Alex looked carefully at her index finger. She decided to risk it.

Ouch. Sure enough, it hurt, and it was softer than the rest of her mouth.

Alex wiped the finger on her jeans.

The mold was spreading. She was getting soft and rotten, just like that peach. If only Alex had paid more attention in class. How long did it take a person to mold up completely and die from rot?

She rummaged among the junk on the car floor and found the tissue box. She rubbed her finger with the tissue. Then she looked at the balled-up tissue, trying to decide what to do with it.

"Are you okay?" asked Mom.

Alex shrugged as she shoved the dirty tissue in her pocket.

"So what seems to be the problem?" Dr. Susan wore a nice smile and a pretty purple coat.

Alex was terrified.

"She's been complaining about her front tooth," said Mom, "and this morning I saw a black spot on it."

"Alex," asked Dr. Susan, "which front tooth is bothering you?"

"The only one I have left," said Alex as she opened her mouth.

"I can see there's been some good tooth wiggling going on here." Dr. Susan put a little mirror inside Alex's mouth.

No makeup flavor.

"Hmm." She adjusted the light so it pointed into Alex's mouth. "I'm pretty sure what the problem is, but we'll take a picture to make sure."

More waiting. A woman came and put a heavy apron on Alex before taking a picture with a funny camera.

"I'll need just a few minutes to get this developed."

Alex's mother scooted over to Alex on her stool and reached for Alex's hand. Alex reached back.

As mothers went, she was a good one.

She hardly ever yelled. She was usually fair. She liked to play games. And Alex was sure that when she died Mom would miss her very, very much.

Alex tried not to cry.

Mom squeezed her hand. She, too, looked like she was about to cry.

Alex squeezed back.

Mom didn't have pretty fingernails, like Jana's mother. Or a pretty accent, like Megan's mother. And unlike Allison's mother, Mom was always on time.

And some parents just pretended to listen. Mom really listened. At least when she wasn't busy.

Alex looked at her mother's soft face. She didn't wear makeup. "I get enough paint on me by accident," she liked to say, "without slopping it on on purpose." She had big green eyes and a small chin and lots of long dark hair, which she usually tied up in a ponytail, sometimes under a bandanna. She wore cool jewelry and clothes. Penelope wore her things all the time. Alex couldn't wait to be old enough.

She swallowed hard. Maybe she would at least make it to her birthday.

"Don't look so sad." Mom ruffled Alex's hair. "No one ever died of a toothache."

63

"Just as I suspected." Dr. Susan came in and snapped the X ray into a little holder. A light came on and there were teeth. Lots of teeth. "Alex's front tooth is dead."

Dead. Already. It was worse than she had thought. Alex forced herself to pay attention.

"Did she ever have a bad fall on it?" asked Dr. Susan.

Mom shrugged her shoulders and looked at Alex. Alex shook her head.

"No matter," said the dentist. "That black spot on the back of the tooth is a hole. The inside of the tooth is dead, and the hole extends up into the root." She pointed at a blob on the picture. "This"—she pointed at a bigger blob—"is your new grown-up tooth that's going to come in there. Because we don't want the infection to compromise the permanent tooth, this primary tooth will have to come out."

"That shouldn't be a problem," said Mom. "Her teeth are falling like rain."

"I mean today. Now." She flipped off the light and turned to Alex.

"Alex, I'm going to give your tooth some sleepy juice. And then I'm going to take it out for you. The sleepy juice is really powerful stuff, so you won't feel a thing. Do either of you have any questions?"

"I thought," Mom said, "that a tooth turns gray when it's dead."

"Sometimes. Sometimes not. Alex?"

"You mean there's no mold on my tooth?"

"Mold?" Dr. Susan stopped her smile halfway.

"Sweetheart," said Mom, "whatever gave you the idea of mold?"

She thought about telling them about Mrs. Newsome and the peach and the cheese, but decided it was too hard to explain. "You mean I'm not going to die?"

"Absolutely not," said Dr. Susan.

Alex was not convinced. "What's this bump by the tooth?"

"That is a little bit of infection from the dead

tooth." Dr. Susan started to get out her tray of tools. "It'll go away in a day or two."

"Alex does seem to be losing her teeth awfully quickly," said Mom. "I don't remember Penelope or Toby losing them all at once like this."

"It often happens that kids lose all their incisors pretty quickly." She tapped her front teeth. "That's four on the bottom, and four on top. Then nature usually gives you a break of a couple years before you lose the cuspids."

Alex nodded. "My other insiders are loose."

"Looks like you won't be eating any corn on the cob for a while."

Alex tried not to look at the tools on the tray. She wasn't dying. But she *was* going to get her tooth pulled. Maybe it was just as bad.

"I'm dabbing a bit of sleepy juice right here with a swab. It might taste a little funny."

It did taste funny. Not at all like makeup. Sort of . . . ugh . . . more tingly than sleepy.

Without even knowing why, Alex started to cry.

"I need to get back to school. Can we do this tomorrow?"

"It won't take long." Dr. Susan reached for something.

Alex closed her eyes. "So, Alex," said Mom, "what do you want to do after we get out of here?"

"Ah on't ow."

"Open wide," Dr. Susan whispered as she put something up to Alex's mouth.

"Maybe we could go for ice cream or frozen yogurt."

"We need just a few minutes for that sleepy juice to work," said Dr. Susan as she patted Alex's hand. "I'll be right back."

"Or we could go home and I can make your favorite vanilla pudding."

Alex glanced at the instruments. In a few minutes Dr. Susan was going to yank out her tooth.

"I got a new card commission, and I was hoping you could help me come up with an idea." She didn't wait for Alex to say anything. "A birth announcement. It's twins! One boy and one girl, not born yet, but the parents want something really special."

Mom was trying to distract her.

"I've done so many baby announcements I could use a little help. Though I guess I haven't done any for boy-girl twins. . . ."

Alex stared as her mother blabbed away. It seemed that suddenly Alex's eyes had developed water faucets.

Dr. Susan appeared. "How we doing here?"

Alex shrugged.

"Feel kind of tingly?"

"My lip is fat."

"Good." She touched something in Alex's mouth. "Feel that?"

"No." Alex wiped her eyes with her left hand. Mom was still holding the right.

"Wonderful. It'll just take a second."

Her chair started leaning backward.

"I've done this a jillion times—a few thousand, anyway—so I'm definitely an expert."

Alex opened her mouth.

"Think about something good," said Mom, "like ice cream, or Dingbat, or painting a picture, or doing a cartwheel, or spending the night with the Regulars, or getting your own room or . . ."

Alex did not want to think about having her own room. She didn't even want her own room.

She kept her eyes closed tight. It didn't hurt, but she didn't want to think about what it did feel like. The best thing Alex could think of was that she was going to get another letter from the Tooth Fairy. Though she would have to write a letter first.

There were so many things to wonder about. Alex had to find out everything about fairy life before her insiders were all out. Where did the Tooth Fairy live? How old was she? How did she know when to come? Alex tried to imagine the prettiest fairy she could, with wings, of course, a sort of glittery costume with a halo of sparkles and—

"There!"

Alex opened her eyes. Mom and Dr. Susan were smiling. Dr. Susan helped her rinse and put a piece of cotton in her mouth.

Alex climbed into the front seat. They were supposed to take turns up front, but it always seemed like Penelope and Toby got more turns.

"I was proud of you, sweetheart. I know it's scary to have a tooth pulled."

Alex looked at the tooth, with its little hole in the back, and then at her mother. Mom would know what to ask the Tooth Fairy, but . . .

Even though she was a very good mother, an excellent mother in fact, Alex couldn't tell her about the Tooth Fairy. She couldn't tell anyone, not even the Regulars. She couldn't risk doing anything that might mess up the magic. Magic had rules, Alex knew, and even though she didn't know exactly what they were, she had to be very careful not to break them.

Alex sat in the corner of her very clean closet to write her letter.

Dear Tuth Ferry,

   Maybe you already know this. Maybe not. I will explain.

   There's a little hole in this tooth. It's not mold. It's not cause I brushed bad. It's cause when I was three I was jumping back and forth between my bed and Penelope's bed and hit my mouth on something. Mom forgot about it. I forgot about it. Penelope says it really happened.

   I will be eight in fifty-nine days and am more careful now. Do you know the way to California? Do you come for birthdays?

   Love,
                Alexis Beatrice Vandershoot

P.S. Here is my school picture, even though I look different with no teeth. Can I have your picture?

71

Alex lay in bed, her tooth gone, her mouth not hurting, not molding to death. Still she couldn't go to sleep.

It wasn't late yet. Penelope wasn't even in bed.

Still Alex was restless. She ran her tongue over the big empty space in front of her mouth.

She couldn't imagine what it would be like to go to sleep in a different room. To have Dad work in the roofing business with her uncle and grandfather. To have a different address and phone number . . . a dog.

The door opened.

"Penelope?"

"Um."

"It's okay if you turn on the light."

Alex squinted as Penelope flipped the switch.

"Penelope, do you think Dad really wants a dog? Or do you think it's a bribe?"

"I don't know, Alex." Penelope buttoned her nightgown. "Does it matter? I mean, we want a dog; they said we could get a dog. So that's good."

"I guess so," said Alex slowly. This was complicated. "But if we do something, Mom and Dad always want to know *why* before they decide if it's good or bad. Like am I cleaning up to be nice or because I want something?"

Penelope brushed her hair. "Do you know what obsessive means?"

Alex shook her head.

"It means taking one thing and never leaving it alone, like a dog with a bone. That's the way you are." She kept brushing her hair. "Just try not to worry so much, Al."

"Easy for you to say. You *want* to move to California."

Penelope didn't say anything, just kept brushing.

"Why do you want to go, anyway?"

"Everything's better in California, Alex. The future is there, the boys are cuter, they have a beach."

"Doesn't Texas have a beach, too?"

"Yeah, but it's far away, so it doesn't count." Penelope snapped off the light.

"Are we gonna live by the beach there, Penelope? Are we? Did Mom tell you that?"

Penelope sighed as she climbed into bed. "My friends complain about their sisters trying to steal their makeup or clothes. You, Alex, will annoy me to death with questions."

Alex closed her eyes and tried to think what it would be like to be the oldest. No handy downs. No teachers telling you how happy they are to have you because of your brother or sister. No brush on the dresser when you couldn't find yours. No interesting big-sister things to show your friends. A *real* babysitter when your parents were out.

No one to remember things about you, like when you jumped on the bed and hit your tooth.

Dear Alexis,
*   Sorry, I don't come for birthdays.*
Teeth are pretty much all I can manage.
Of course I know the way to California.
Don't you think kids there lose teeth? I
look forward to all my visits to you, Alex,
no matter where you are.
*   What a lovely picture. It's so nice to*

74

have something from you, since I'm letting you keep your teeth. Sorry, can't trade though. One of the special things about fairies is that we can't be photographed. My appearance is also changeable. Sometimes I'm especially beautiful, fairy dust and all that. At other times I am more ordinary looking and could, in fact, pass for someone's mother.

Wonderful job on that closet, Alex. Do you think if I came to visit your mother she could do that to hers? Probably not. Your mother is pretty hopeless in the cleaning department. I personally think that chart of hers is just an excuse to get out of doing the work.

Love,
The Tooth Fairy

Chapter 5

The microwave oven? The clothes hamper? The dryer? Yes, the dryer.

For days Alex had been trying to decide where to hide her Tooth Fairy letters during the move. No one would look in the dryer, all closed up in the big truck. The letters couldn't get lost, they couldn't burn up, and Alex could be sure to be there when they got the dryer off the truck. But . . .

Then she wouldn't have them either.

Alex got the letters out and read them to herself almost every day, studying the little paintings on the envelopes, the fancy writing, the words of encouragement. The secret things that no one else knew about her. Beatrice. Alex never told *anyone* her middle name.

No, she couldn't bear to be without them in the car, even if that meant discovery was more likely.

"Alex," called Mom, "the Regulars are here."

Cool. Alex started to run, until she was faced with the hallway crammed with boxes. Stacked with boxes. Alex turned sideways and scooched toward her friends.

"Hi, guys!"

"Hi," they each said, and hugged her in turn.

Alex didn't like that at all. They hardly ever hugged. She had hugged Jana when she had an accident at school. And they all hugged Allison when her dad was in the hospital. Those were the only Regular hugs Alex could remember.

They all sat around the kitchen table. Waiting for something.

"You want to play Monopoly?" asked Alex. Toby had taught them, and they loved it—all that money, and those cute little houses.

"Sure," said Jana. "Monopoly sounds good."

"Sorry," said Alex's mother from over a box, "the games are all packed."

"What about hide-and-seek?" said Alex. "That's not packed. And it's fun hiding in all the empty closets."

"Almost forgot," said Megan. "We brought you a present."

"A present?" Alex had gotten them each something, but it had not occurred to her that they would do the same.

Shyly, Allison held out a wrapped package.

As she took it, Alex noticed that the three of them were sitting, together, on the opposite side of the table.

The wrapping paper was blue, with specks of silver in it, something the Tooth Fairy might like. Alex tried wiggling her teeth with her tongue. Not nearly loose enough.

"Go ahead," said Jana. "Open it."

Alex popped the tape and slowly opened the paper. It was a book with a pretty flowered cover.

"It's an address book," said Megan.

"And we all wrote our names and addresses in for you," said Jana.

"So you won't forget us," said Allison.

Alex smiled. At least with her face. She knew what she was supposed to say. "I'll never forget you." She never *would* forget them, but it made her throat ache the way they were treating her, not Regular at all, but like she was different from the rest of them. "Thank you," she said, and went to get their presents from the otherwise empty pantry.

They were big, lumpy packages, and Alex smiled happily as she handed them to her friends.

Jana was always fastest. "Thank you, Alex, these are great."

"Yes. Thank you," said Megan and Allison.

And they all hugged her *again*.

Alex tried to think of something Regular to say. "Did you notice how the last week of school the Lisa Girls were all bringing sunflower seeds? But these are *flavored* sunflower seeds, barbecue. I bet the Lisa Girls don't have those."

80

Megan examined the label on her bag.

"They were the biggest bags we could find," said Alex. "I bet there's more than one thousand seven hundred seeds in those bags."

They sat at the table, staring at one another.

Alex wanted to play, to run, to have everything be regular. She wanted to get in those giant boxes in the backyard, to stand in her parents' empty closet and try and hear the echo. "So, how about that game of hide and seek?"

"What time is it?" asked Jana.

Did that matter? Alex leaned over to look at the oven clock. "It's two fifty-two."

"My mom's going to pick us up in a few minutes," said Allison. "We're going to a movie and have an overnight at my house."

Megan gave Allison a shove.

Alex worked very hard to keep her face Regular.

"Sorreee," Allison looked at Megan. "Alex, I wanted you to come, but Mama said you'd want to spend your last night at home."

Did she want to? Could she use the word "want" for anything that was going on right now?

"Anyone like a pickle?" asked Mom. "Or how about some applesauce? Or blackberry jam . . . or crackers? I've got all kinds of odds and ends that are begging to get eaten up."

"No, thank you, Mrs. Vandershoot," said Allison. "I'm saving up for popcorn."

Megan shoved her again.

"I'd love a pickle," said Jana. "Are they dill pickles?"

"Yes, they're dill pickles." Alex's mother set the jar and some paper towels on the table. "Sorry, all the forks and plates are packed. Alex, could you please come help me with something in the other room?"

Alex followed her to the living room.

"I'm sure they didn't mean to hurt your feelings," Mom whispered. "If you like, I can tell Allison's mother that you'd like to come along."

Alex thought about the three of them on the

opposite side of the table, about her sleeping bag that was already packed. Being mad at them felt both horrible and not so bad. Maybe she would cry less. "That's okay. I'll stay here."

A couple of minutes later they were gone, really gone.

Alex helped her mom figure out how to fit the cereal into a big carton. "Where is everybody?"

"Well, your father is closing our bank accounts and making sure we have enough money for the trip. Penelope is at Vicky's, and Toby will be back soon. He wants to wheel the dolly." She wedged a bag of rice into an empty space.

"Mom, can I ask you something?"

"Sure." She wrote KITCHEN on the side of the box, taped it shut, then stood up to look at Alex.

"Do you think the Tooth Fairy might come even if I didn't lose a tooth? If it was an emergency?"

She stared at Alex. "I don't know. You can try."

Alex nodded. "Can I borrow some of your paint and nice paper?"

"Sorry, sweetheart, everything's packed." Mom pulled the chart off the refrigerator door, smushed it into a ball, and heaved it in the trash.

Alex went to her naked bedroom. The pictures were off the walls and all her clothes and toys were packed. She checked her bag for the car and made sure her Tooth Fairy letters were underneath Tiny, Alberta, and Dingbat, where she could get them easily. She would be careful, of course, but Alex had decided that the risk of discovery by Toby was not too great.

Alex smoothed out the pretty wrapping paper from her address book, then carefully tore it in two. Half she folded into a sort of envelope. The other half she turned over to use as writing paper.

Dear Tuth Ferry,
    Sorry but none of my teeth were loose enough. Maybe you already know why I'm writing. Maybe not. We're moving. In the morning. To California. A bunch of workers are

helping put everything in the truck. The best part is, we get to stay in a motel on the way.

I don't have friends anymore. I'd really like some in California. Can you help me? Uncle Matthew found us a house. Penelope is so happy. Dad says she gets her own room. Does that mean I have my own room to? I am afraid to ask. Maybe I could give my room to Mom since she wants one for work.
Love,
Alexis Beatrice Vandershoot

P.S. What do you do in the day?

Alex read her letter again. The writing was a little crooked and the words got bigger toward the bottom, but it was a good letter. The paper made it look fancy. Still she felt bad. No tooth. The Tooth Fairy would be very disappointed, if she came at all.

Alex went to the kitchen and got a strip of packing tape and a piece of plain packing paper.

"Alex," said Mom, "I don't want your bags to end up in the truck by accident. Go put them with the stuff for the car."

There was a man in her room.

"Sorry, peach." He lifted up the nightstand. "Didn't mean to scare you."

"Are you guys taking everything?"

"Everything but the beds. Get those in the A.M. before you head out."

Alone again, Alex stared at the front lawn. There were the washer and the dryer, and living-room furniture, and thirty-seven boxes with the names of rooms written on them. It was very weird.

Alex sat in the corner of her bed facing the wall and carefully folded a fortune-teller. It wasn't as pretty as one made with origami paper, but she used her best handwriting for the numbers and fortunes, then tucked the fortune-teller into the wrapping-paper envelope and sealed it with the tape.

✳

There were so many sounds. The cicadas. Her ceiling fan. The squeak of the bed when she moved. Her parents talking in the kitchen. Penelope breathing. The air conditioner.

The house in California didn't have an air conditioner. Imagine that. "How tacky," Toby had said when he found out. "I'm not living in no dump without air conditioning." Dad got really mad then, said Toby had no say at all where they lived, and besides, the house didn't have air conditioning because in California you didn't need air conditioning. Imagine that!

Alex looked nervously at the slightly open window. It was strictly against the rules to open the window when it was hot and the air conditioner was on. She hated breaking the rules. Something else to worry about.

Penelope was snoring now. It wasn't a bad snore, as snores went.

Did the Tooth Fairy make a noise when she came in? Press with her little fairy foot on the squeaky board near the dresser, or where the dresser used to be? Did she shuffle the covers? Flip on the light?

Alex was very sure *she* wouldn't flip on the light. She could probably see in the dark.

There were always so many questions Alex wanted to ask when she wasn't writing a letter. It was different when she had the pencil in her hand, scarier. The questions flew out of her mind, like birds. It was hard to know what was okay to ask. What the rules of politeness were when it came to fairies. Alex yawned and slipped her hand under her pillow.

It was still dark when they woke her up.

"Sorry, sweetheart," said Mom. "We want to get an early start."

Alex was only one quarter awake.

"Let's get up now. I'm going to put all the sheets in a plastic bag, so we can get your bed in the truck."

"Wait." Alex was all the way awake now. She put her hand under the pillow and closed it around a plain piece of paper.

She held it tightly in her hand until they were
in the car.

Dear Alexis,
    Congratulations on moving. I think
you get your own room. You'll like it once
you get used to it. Don't worry about your
mother. Maybe she'll get a room, too.
    Friends are harder. The best way to
have friends is to be a friend. Keep me
posted.
    I sleep in the daytime, silly.
    Thanks for the fortune-teller. I really
liked my fortune: "You get one night with
no teeth at all."
                        Love,
                            The Tooth Fairy

Chapter 6

On the map, the states didn't look big at all. But when you were in the middle of one it went on for hours and hours. And the only good thing was when the car ran low on gas and then you got to go to the bathroom. Big whoop. But you went even if you didn't have to, because you wanted to get out of the car and because it would be a long time until you got to go again.

Alex wiggled her newest loose tooth, the top insider on the right.

"Q!" yelled Penelope and Toby at the same time.

"It's mine," Toby said.

"No, I saw it first," said Penelope.

91

They were trying to find each letter of the alphabet on signs or license plates.

Alex had started playing with them, but gave up at K.

"How far to California?" she asked.

"Well . . ." said Dad. "I don't think it's California you care about. It's Stockdale."

Stockdale. What a funny name for a town.

"We enter California at the south and then drive north to Stockdale. With the stop at Yosemite, we'll be on the road five or six more days."

Didn't they know that the only day that mattered was today? July seventeenth. She was eight years old *today,* and no one had even mentioned it. Alex wiggled her tooth.

Toby and Penelope were now stuck on V. At least they'd have an easy time with Z. It was on every Arizona license plate they passed.

Alex wiggled her tooth. There wasn't anything else to do, and besides, she had an idea about the Tooth Fairy she wanted to test out.

"Is it time for lunch?" Toby asked as they slowed slightly.

"Yes," said Mom. "We thought we'd go to a super-market and get stuff for a picnic to celebrate Alex's birthday."

Alex smiled.

They kept stopping for directions. First to find a market, then twice to find a park.

Mom set out the barbecued chicken and the watermelon, and potato salad. There was a Pepper Farm cake and a little box with candles.

Alex paid most attention, however, to the three littie wrapped boxes that Dad set next to the cake. It wasn't the same as a regular party, but presents were presents.

Lunch was delicious. The potato salad had little crunchy things that made it especially good. And because it was her birthday, no one made a face when she took a third serving. The watermelon was good even if it wasn't cold, and the chicken—she got the drumstick without even having to fight for it. So what if the juice was all over her face? That just made it taste better.

Mom cut her another piece of chicken.

Ugh. There was a hard piece of gristle or something.

Alex smiled inside as she realized that her tooth had fallen out right in her mouth. She was just about to tell everyone when she changed her mind, and she secretly slipped the tooth in her pocket.

"Anybody want cake?" asked Mom as she unboxed the cake and poked in the candles.

"Anybody not want cake?" asked Penelope, and she ruffled Alex's hair.

"Do we have to sing?" asked Toby.

"Of course we get to sing," Mom said.

And sing they did. Loudly.

Alex got all the candles in one breath.

She had been suspicious when Mom pulled the Pepper Farm cake out of the freezer at the store—"I've always wanted to try one of these," she said—but Alex was pleasantly surprised. It didn't taste like

94

pepper at all. It tasted like regular chocolate. With little wax bits on the top.

She tried not to open her mouth too far so no one would notice her tooth, but they weren't paying attention anyway.

Cake gone, Mom set the presents in front of Alex.

She knew to open the card first.

"To my favorite . . ."

On the front of the card was a drawing of a girl. It looked exactly like her. Except for the hair. The hair was a wild tangle of brightly colored skinny little ribbons. Alex's own hair was straight, but she loved the card just the same.

She read it again, "To my favorite . . ."—she opened it—"eight-year-old! Happy Birthday. Love, Mom and Dad."

Alex turned it over. Sure enough, there was Mom's special design—a logo, she called it—with the three Cs for Carol's Custom Cards on the back.

"Thanks, Mom." Alex kissed her.

"You're welcome." She set the presents in front of Alex.

Alex waited a minute so this best part would last a little longer. Being afraid to ask for something too expensive, she hadn't asked for anything at all.

Carefully Alex opened a book-shaped package. It was from Toby and Penelope.

A box of stationery, complete with a set of stickers so she could add flowers of all different kinds to the leaves that were already printed on the paper. It was beautiful.

"We thought you'd be writing a lot of letters to your friends," said Toby.

"Thanks, guys. It's really pretty."

She turned to the next box. It was a container of bubble bath from her grandparents. She couldn't quite remember what they looked like. She'd see them again soon enough. Mom had bought the bubble bath herself and put their names on it.

Mom said, "You have to—"

"I know. I know." Alex tapped the stationery.

The third box was more interesting. It rattled. A lot. And it had a sort of plastic-y sound through the wrapping paper. Please don't let it be a baby toy, she thought. She popped the tape and pulled the paper off. It was a game. A travel game.

"Connect For," she read. "Connect for what? That doesn't make any sense."

"It's like ticktacktoe," said Mom. "Only you use these little checker guys and instead of three, you want to get four in a row."

"Oh!" Alex looked at the box again, then slapped her forehead. "Connect *Four*."

"Right," said Dad.

"It looks like a good game." Alex stirred the baby checkers. "And now I have a surprise for you."

Alex smiled really big with her top lip and reached into her pocket.

Everyone stared at her mouth.

"On your birthday!" Dad hugged her. "How appropriate."

"Good going," said Toby.

97

They all hugged, and it turned out to be not such a bad birthday.

Toby and Penelope wanted to play Connect Four with her in the car. Since it was a two-person game, they started an argument over who was going to play first.

"You two play it together first," said Alex.

Mom looked at her weirdly.

Alex did want to play. Just not right now. "I like the game, Mom. Isn't it okay if they go first?"

"Fine. Fine." Mom shrugged and turned around front.

Alex had some planning to do. It would be so much easier if she could get out the letters and look at them. She wanted to touch them, hold them, but she couldn't do that.

Alex looked wistfully at the new stationery and all the fancy stickers. She wouldn't use that either. The motel last night had some ugly postcards and writing paper in the rickety desk. Maybe the one tonight would, too.

By the time they pulled into the Sands Motel in Empire, Arizona, Alex had practically composed the letter in her head.

Dear Tooth Fairy,

Sorry I have been spelling your name wrong all this time.

You said you don't come for birthdays, but gess what? It's my birthday and I lost a tooth. Mom says you will always know where to find me. I hope that is true because I don't even know where to find me.

That's a joke. We are staying in a motel with green bedspreads and little tiny towels. Mom and Dad get one bed. Penelope and I get one bed. Toby gets the rollaway bed. He is a boy.

Have you ever played Connect Four? It's fun. I can beat Toby sometimes. Sometimes Toby can

beat Penelope. So maybe tomorrow
I can beat Penelope sometimes.
None of us can beat Mom. Dad won't
play. Even when Mom's driving.

Vacation is fun. It would be more
fun if we were going back home at
the end.

What do you like for breakfast?
Maybe I can fix you blueberry muffins
sometime. I learned how just before
we left.

Love,
Alexis Beatrice Vandershoot

P.S. Toby has a loose tooth. Do you
write him letters, too?

The squeak of the rollaway bed woke Alex up.
She snatched the letter from under her pillow and
raced Toby for the bathroom. He won.

Alex stared at the envelope in her hand. It was
from here, the Sands Motel, Empire, Arizona.

Alexis Beatrice Vandershoot

Alex smiled.

She was right.

The first couple of letters were so exciting Alex had imagined the Tooth Fairy in her castle—or wherever she lived—writing Alex a note with a fancy pen made out of a feather. But the more Alex thought about it, the more that didn't make sense.

The Tooth Fairy wouldn't have time to read Alex's letter, go home, write a letter, then come back.

The Tooth Fairy wrote her letters right here, in the same room with Alex.

That explained why the first few letters were so

101

fancy. She had borrowed Mom's card-making stuff. But for the last letter at home everything was packed, so the Tooth Fairy used plain paper. And this time she had used the paper from the Sands Motel. There was no seal either.

It gave Alex a shiver to know the Tooth Fairy didn't just flit in and out. She sat here and looked at Alex, thinking about her and what to write. She sat at a desk just like a real person.

"Toby." Alex knocked on the bathroom door. "You about done?"

"Just a minute, I've got to finish shaving."

"Well, hurry up." She couldn't stay mad at him. " 'Cause I've got to put my makeup on."

Toby opened the door. Alex held the letter behind her back and slipped into the bathroom.

Dear Alexis,
> *Congratulations. A birthday and a lost tooth. What a special day.*
> *Don't worry about spelling my name*

102

wrong before. But it is always exciting to me to see my children learn new things. And you know what? It's hard to tell, what with you being under the covers and all, but I do believe you've grown.

I am glad to hear that you're learning to cook. For breakfast I favor Starlight Soufflé or Floating Islands, light foods that won't interfere with my flying.

No, I haven't ever written Toby a letter. Then again, he's never written me one. Most kids, Alexis, just want their money. It is the rare child who thinks about me as much as I do her.

Love,

The T.F.

Chapter 7

Dear Tooth Fairy,

A new house is like a new pair of shoes. It may be nice, nicer in some ways than what you had before, but it sure doesn't feel good.

Penelope lets me sleep on the floor of her room so I don't get—

The front door opened.

"Alex!" called Peggy.

Alex quickly folded the paper and put it in her pocket.

She couldn't get used to no knocking. Everyone in Texas knocked. Even if you were friends. And lived next door.

But Peggy's mom didn't knock, Peggy didn't knock, and when Alex went to Peggy's house, she didn't knock either. And she didn't ask before helping herself to an apple. Cookies, yes. You always had to ask about cookies, but anything else was okay, and they'd only known the Leatherbys for three weeks.

"Over here, Peggy, in Mom's roomlet."

Peggy skipped over and propped her elbows on Mom's worktable, where Alex had been writing. "What's a roomlet?"

"That's what Mom calls this. Not quite a room, I guess." Alex looked at the corner of the sun room where all of Mom's papers and paints and card-making stuff was stacked in perfect order against the wall. It was the only part of the house that was neat.

"You want to go play at the school?" Peggy asked.

"Nah, I don't want to go to the new school."

"It's not really new," said Peggy. "It's just new to you."

Alex shrugged.

"How about turning on some music, shoving back all the furniture, and doing gymnastics?" said Peggy. "Or we could make some sandwiches and go to the park for a picnic."

"Better. Or we could build a playhouse," offered Alex, "and have our picnic inside."

"Build a playhouse?"

"Come on, I'll show you."

Before she went into Penelope's room that night, Alex unfolded her note. She put a sticker of a rose underneath where she was writing before.

> Peggy Leatherby is the best thing
> about Stockdale. I had to dump out
> six boxes to find the close pins, but
> we made the best house ever. We

used all the sheets, even the ones
from Mom and Dad's bed and took
up almost the whole downstairs. (All
us kids wanted a two-storage house,
but it's a pain. Maybe you can teach
me to fly up and down stairs.)

Alex wiggled her loosest tooth, the top one on
the left. No luck. How long before she could put
this letter under her pillow? But she was writing it
anyway because she didn't want to forget.

We had tuna sandwiches and
soup and pudding in our playhouse
and get this. Hope you don't mind I
called the pudding Starlight Soufflé.
Then Peggy came up with Dragon's
Breath Stew for the vegetable soup
and Mermaid Surprise for the tuna
sandwiches. Peggy has great ideas
and her room is even more messy

than mine, except I have an excuse
cause we just moved.

Alex thought about crossing out the part about her messy room but didn't.

She tucked the unfinished letter in the bottom of her underwear drawer, got Dingbat, Alberta, and Tiny, and went into Penelope's room to sleep on the floor.

"Come on, Alex." Mom brushed her hair. "We're going to get you some school clothes."

"I don't need any school clothes. I don't want any school clothes."

"Alex, your pants are creeping up your legs. And it might be nice to have at least one dress in your closet."

"I can wear Penelope's handy downs. They're already broken in."

"Yes, but—"

"Besides, you can't afford it."

"Come over here and sit down," said Mom.

The two of them sat at the empty kitchen table. It was weird not to have Mom's work stuff spread everywhere.

"Stop worrying!" Mom said. "I am the mother. It's my job, and I want you to look forward to being a third-grader. Your father has a job in the family business now, you know that. We can afford to buy you clothes. The only thing you need to worry about is playing house with Peggy."

Alex doodled with her finger on the sticky table. Mom had been so busy for so long Alex couldn't remember the last time she'd forced Alex to talk. Alone.

Alex looked up. "How about if I look forward to playing with Peggy and worry about the new school?"

"I'm sorry." Mom set down her keys. "The new school didn't occur to me, sweetie. Penelope and Toby aren't upset about it, and I figured this should be easier for you because you're younger."

Alex didn't say anything.

"You know what? It's natural to be worried. It's

okay to be worried. I'd be worried about you if you *weren't* worried.

"But you should remember this, that you'll worry and worry, and then suddenly the first day of school will be here, and soon you'll wonder what all that worrying was about." Mom leaned over and kissed Alex on the forehead. "Don't use up all your worries now. One day, you may really need them."

Alex sat there, trying to figure out why those words were so familiar.

Alex smoothed the rumpled letter on her desk.

There are some good things about having my own room.
1) I don't have to hide in the closet to write to you.
2) The clothes on the floor are my clothes, not Penelope's.
That's all I can think of now. Maybe more later.
I wrote to Jana, Allison, and

111

Megan. But none of them wrote back.
I'm glad you write back.

My new clothes are okay, but I'm
trying to make them softer. I put them
under my covers and Peggy and I
jumped on the bed. Softly.

Alex pulled out a second piece of paper and put
a pansy sticker and a tulip sticker on it.

Toby is camping with Uncle Matt.
The house is very quiet.

Alex reached up to wiggle her tooth.

And it fell out. Just like that.

All of her wondering and wondering and wiggling and wiggling, and it finally just fell out. In her
hand.

Alex was about to run and tell everyone. But she
decided to finish her letter first.

Her tooth sat there on the desk. It seemed to be

winking at her. Suddenly the letter and what she wanted to say were much more important. She drew a small flower on the corner of her paper. Then she made it a bouquet.

I'm really excited because my tooth just came out. Do you get excited about things? Do you ever have to move? Is it weird to miss your brother when he's gone even though when he's here you usually don't like him? Do you think it's okay to have one really really best friend?
Love,
Alexis Beatrice Vandershoot

That night Alex slept in her own room for the first time.

She didn't even have a hard time going to sleep. A warm, cozy feeling seemed to be coming up from under her pillow.

*

"Morning, sweetheart."

Eyes still closed, Alex felt the covers move next to her. Mom never woke her up during the summer. "Is something wrong?"

"Isn't it nice to be able to use a blanket during the summer?" She squeezed under the covers with Alex. "Nothing's wrong. Just thought I'd keep you company for a few minutes."

"Keep me company?" Alex had a small bed.

"I think it's really nice how quickly you're adjusting."

"Adjusting?" Alex was awake enough to realize how weird this was. Breakfast was Mom's favorite meal of the day, the only one she actually cooked. And between cooking breakfast, seeing Dad off, yelling at Penelope to empty the dishwasher, making business calls—"you're more likely to catch people first thing in the morning"—and starting in on the day's unpacking, there was never any quiet time in the morning.

Morning. Suddenly Alex remembered the letter waiting underneath her pillow.

"What's for breakfast, Mom?"

Mom ignored the question. "You are so lucky to have found Peggy."

"I miss my friends in Dallas," Alex said.

"Of course you do. I must like Peggy because she reminds me of you."

Alex eased her hand up under her pillow. There it was. She could feel the texture of the stiff envelope. Alex hoped it was a fancy one this time. She loved the fancy ones.

"I had a best friend once," Mom went on. "I was in the first grade and desperately wanted a friend. This little girl named Lulu Klein looked like good friend material. She had freckles and glasses and she stood on the side of the playground kind of by herself, so I walked up and asked her if she would be my best friend." Mom put her arm around Alex's shoulder.

Alex froze, her hand still beneath her pillow.

"Lulu said yes. And that was it. We were best friends for six years, the whole time we went to Elliot Elementary."

115

"What happened after that?" Alex was curious in spite of herself.

"When we got to junior high we were in different classes." Mom kissed Alex on top of the head. "Lulu and I had so much fun together. Lulu's mother always cooked whatever Lulu wanted for her birthday, so every year we kept coming up with fancier and fancier dinners for her mom to cook. One year we had a roast goose. I still remember those birthdays. Lulu's birthday is May ninth."

Alex needed to ask Peggy when her birthday was.

"We did all kinds of things together. Set up a trading post in our backyard, took painting lessons from Lulu's mother, had a spy club, stayed at each other's houses."

"We've never done any of those things."

"Don't worry, you will," said Mom. "I could arrange the painting classes."

"Not for me." Alex's hand was going to sleep. "Maybe for Toby. He's a good drawer."

116

"He is, isn't he? But you're good at many other things, Alex. Don't ever let anyone take your imagination away from you."

What a silly idea. How would someone take away her imagination? But before she could think about it anymore, Mom got up.

"I'm fixing your favorite breakfast: corn pancakes, cantaloupe, and scrambled eggs. Want to come help?"

"Okay." Alex worked hard to keep her voice regular. "I'll be there in a few minutes."

Alex threw back her pillow. Wow. This one was really fancy.

Her name was in the center, as usual, but the painting was incredible. It looked like a stage, with fancy drapey curtains on the sides and top, and complicated lights at the bottom pointing upward toward her name. It didn't look like regular paint either, but some sort of extra shiny and glittery paint.

Alex carefully broke the seal.

Dear Alexis,

My word, you are filled with questions today. The only problem is, I'm not sure I am filled with answers.

That is a fairy joke, which, I'm afraid, means it is a bad joke. We fairies are known for many things, but, sadly, a sense of humor is not among them. We have to make do with a sense of wonder and

118

believing in the possibilities of life instead.

I know what you mean about new clothes. I don't really start getting comfortable with my fairy outfits until they're at least a couple of hundred years old. Not too sure about jumping on them on the bed, however. Isn't that how you got the hole in that other tooth? Wouldn't it be easier to ask your mother to wash them first? Personally I use fairy dust (new and improved) to wash my things, but I've heard that fabric softener is also good stuff.

No, Alexis, I never have to move. Although I travel a great deal, I've been in the castle now for as long as I can remember. But we redo the gardens or the furniture every hundred years or so to keep it looking fresh.

It's not "weird"—to use a human expression—to miss your brother. That's one good thing about having brothers go away, so you can remember the good things about them. When they are sitting next to you cleaning out their spit valves, it is sometimes hard to remember their good qualities.

Sorry about your Regular friends. Not everyone likes writing letters as much as we do.

Best friends are fine. Peggy seems a good choice. And you seem a good choice for her.

Of course I get excited about things . . . a good updraft makes flying ever so much more fun. Stardust tea cakes positively set my wings a-quiver, and most of all I get terribly happy whenever I hear that Alexis Beatrice Vandershoot has lost a tooth.

Love,
The T.F.

Chapter 8

Alex and Peggy dropped their book bags on the steamer trunk in the doorway and raced Toby to the kitchen. Toby won by a cookie. The phone rang.

"Mom," called Alex, "it's Dad."

Mom picked it up in the other room.

"Don't you just adore Mr. H?" Alex said. His last name was Higginbotham, but everyone called him Mr. H.

"Adore." Peggy licked the center out of her cookie. "We're lucky. The kids in Mrs. Williams's class have been complaining about her for months."

"That's amazing," said Toby, "since we've only been in school for three weeks."

"Not amazing at all." Peggy scrunched up her face at him. "They started complaining *before* school started."

Alex and Peggy laughed at her joke.

"Ouch." Alex's tooth hurt as she bit on a cookie.

"Alex," called Mom, "you got a card today from Texas."

Alex and Peggy dashed to her worktable, where Alex's mom was searching through her papers. "I know I put it here."

Alex watched her mother look for the card. "Is Dad okay?"

"Of course he's okay." She kept shuffling. "Why?"

"Dad never used to call home during the day."

"Aha!" She handed Alex the card. "He didn't? I guess you're right. Maybe he's not under the same pressure working here."

"It's only a postcard." Alex stared at it with disappointment.

The front of the card was a baby wearing a diaper, a cowboy hat, and boots. The cartoon bubble said A BIG HOWDY FROM LIL TEX! Alex turned the card over.

Dear Alex,
    We are fine. How are you? Jana got a fish. School is fine.
            Love,
                Megan, Jana, Allison

That's it? Alex couldn't believe it. She had written them two letters apiece. That was six letters in all, on her fancy paper. She had drawn them pictures of the new house and saved the sunflower stickers for them and written especially to Megan about how it wasn't that bad having to move. Alex's eyes started to hurt. She moved her index finger across the card, counting. Just nineteen words. And that included their names. It was so . . . so Regular.

She looked up.

Mom and Peggy were staring.

"They signed it 'love,'" said Mom.

Alex shrugged. "Let's go to my room, Peggy."

They sat on the bed.

"I'm so glad you moved here. And I hope you never move away." Peggy paused. "But if you do, I'll write you a real letter every week. Until I die."

What a promise. "And I'll write you back." Alex smiled. "As long as there's a post office."

"You want to build another house? We might need to use tape"—Peggy looked at the walls—"but I bet we could cover up your whole room."

"Maybe later." Alex checked to make sure the door was closed. "I want to show you something." Alex walked over to her dresser, reached beneath her underwear, and pulled out the letters. They were stacked neatly and tied with a ribbon. She handed Peggy the bundle.

Peggy's eyes were question marks, but she didn't say anything as she carefully undid the ribbon and opened the first letter.

Alex smiled inside. She hadn't *decided* to show Peggy the precious letters. It wasn't like that at all. The thought had only just occurred to her, and the second it did, she acted upon it.

Peggy's eyes went from question marks to exclamation points.

"Wow," said Peggy, "this is incredible." She was on the fourth letter—the one about not being photographed and what a good job Alex had done on her closet.

Alex had read them so many times that she practically had them memorized.

Peggy kept reading, fingering the paper gently as she went.

Alex would never have shown the Regulars the letters. She didn't know why, exactly, but she knew it with all her heart.

Peggy studied the sixth letter, the one written on Alex's birthday. "Look at this," said Peggy, pointing to the return address. There was a line through the Sands Motel, and in its place was written *Tooth*

Fairy Castle, One Stardust Lane, Land of Enchant-ment.

Alex stared. She couldn't believe she hadn't noticed. That there could be anything about the letters she didn't know. Then again, she had focused on the actual letters, the jokes, the clues, the interesting details.

Peggy read the last letter. "Oh, I'm in this one!" she said gleefully. "This is so cool." Peggy reached up to feel her teeth. "Do you think she'd write me a letter?"

Alex shrugged. "I wrote the first time because I wanted to keep my tooth. I never even expected an answer."

Peggy reread the letters.

Alex wiggled her teeth. There were two loose ones on the bottom, on either side of the new middle teeth. One was a definite possibility.

Peggy reached up into her mouth and wiggled. "What have you got?"

"One, maybe." Alex opened wide to show her.

"That's pretty good," Peggy said. "Mine aren't near that loose."

"I've got this idea," said Alex. "You know how little kids leave a snack for Santa Claus?"

Peggy nodded.

"How about if we make cookies for the Tooth Fairy?"

"Great!" Peggy stacked up the letters. "But won't she only come if you have a tooth?"

Alex frowned as she wiggled. "She came once without, but that was kind of an emergency."

"Let me see it." Peggy reached into Alex's mouth and wiggled. "How about if we tie a piece of string to the doorknob and slam the door?"

"Fine, as long as you don't tie the other end to my tooth."

Peggy laughed.

"Let's cook first," said Alex, "and worry about the tooth later."

There was no need for a recipe. They mixed up a marvelous concoction of everything they could think of: chocolate, eggs, flour, more chocolate, sugar, salt, raisins, sunflower seeds (shelled), more flour, several things from small bottles in the spice cabinet, and, of course, more chocolate. In between mixing they took turns wiggling Alex's tooth. While the cookies were baking (Penelope helped with that part), they made up stories about what kind of a life the Tooth Fairy must have, how she could fly as fast as the wind and had a remarkable memory for children and teeth, and a seemingly endless supply of quarters.

"I bet she has a fairy cat and a fairy dog to keep her company," said Peggy, "and she plays games like . . . fairy-tale rummy, or fairy-opoly."

Alex nodded. "But remember she's human looking, too. She sometimes wears overalls, 'could pass for someone's mother,' and knows about laundry."

The timer buzzed.

Carefully they slid the cookies out and put them on an unfolded brown paper bag. To make them cool faster Peggy and Alex blew on them.

The cookies were lumpy, brown, and oddly

shaped. Some were small, some large, and some had bits sticking out in various places. But Alex knew better than to judge food, especially cookies, by their looks.

She and Peggy each held a cookie. They raised the cookies to their mouths at the same time. They bit at the same time.

They ran to the sink at the same time.

"You know," Alex said, after she rinsed her mouth, "I think we need to give the Tooth Fairy *all* of these cookies."

"Good idea."

They arranged them carefully on a plate and took them upstairs to Alex's room. The nightstand had gone to Penelope, so they set the plate on the desk.

"How's your tooth doing?" asked Peggy.

Alex wiggled. It was off in the back. "Not ready yet. How about yours?"

Peggy wiggled. "Not nearly there. I think we need to concentrate on yours. Are you ready to try the thing with the string and the door?"

"How about if we ride bikes instead?"

"Great," said Peggy. "Maybe one of us will fall on our face."

All the kids, even Penelope and Celia, jumped on the giant trampoline while the moms and dads got dinner on the table. Peggy's mother had made rolls and salad, and her father was cooking chicken and hot dogs. Penelope had made deviled eggs, and Alex's mother had fixed baked potatoes with good things to put on them. "It was hard to get near the kitchen this afternoon," she said. "What with all the girls cooking up a storm."

The two families had taken to having dinner together once a week, an arrangement that suited everyone. Even though Toby sometimes got annoyed that the Leatherbys didn't have a son—Celia, their other daughter, was a year older than Penelope—their pool table helped to make up for it.

Although she wiggled as she bounced on the trampoline, Alex was getting frustrated about the tooth. "Why don't you work on yours awhile, Peg?"

"Okay." Peggy wiggled several teeth in turn, as if she were playing a piano.

There were trees in the backyard. No real lawn, but a table next to the deck. The yards were much bigger, and the houses were bigger, too, here, but in a tumbledown way. The Vandershoots' dishwasher worked only part of the time, and the hot-water heater was small. If you were third in line at the bathroom—especially if the washer was going—you'd get a cold shower. The downstairs toilet overflowed every few days and some of the doors didn't close very well.

Alex liked their new house a lot.

She heaped her plate to overflowing. She especially liked dumping lots of stuff on her potato. There was cheese, bacon, onions, broccoli, sunflower seeds, and sour cream. Alex didn't like sour cream—too slimy—but she took everything else.

"Your trampoline is so much fun," she said. "It feels like flying."

Peggy nodded. "I was closing my eyes and it was

131

just like . . ." she whispered. "You know . . ."

Alex did know. She smiled and took a big bite of potato. She was so hungry she hardly wanted to chew. It was only potato, so she didn't worry about it. Chew. Swallow. She was just about to take another bite when she realized something was different. Wrong.

Her tooth was gone.

Dear Tooth Fairy,

Let me introduce myself. My name is Peggy Leatherby. I will be eight next month. Mom says my best point is that I think TV is nonsense. My worst point is that most of the time I think school is nonsense.

I did not lose a tooth. Today.

Alex let me write along with her. And even borrow her pretty paper. Actually not "borrow," since I guess she's not going to get it back.

132

Could you write me, too? I am very interested in fairies and trolls and dragons and stuff like that.

I hope you and your family are doing well.

Sincerely,
Peggy Leatherby

Dear Tooth Fairy,

Hope your not mad I told Peggy about you.

We made you some cookies. Maybe you will like them. Maybe not.

Sorry I don't have my tooth. I swallowed it. Toby says it will come out in my poop. Dad says it will stay there forever, kind of a tummy souvenir. Maybe I don't want to know.

Peggy is staying overnight.

I know you said moving is not your department, but what about staying?

Can you fix it so we can stay in Stockdale forever? Mom said not to worry, that everyone was doing well here, that was the important thing, that if we always worry we can't be happy where we are. I would like a promise. Moving is a very bad thing.

I thought of another bad thing. There's only one more insider tooth to lose. Then it will be years before any more come out. I love you.

Love,
Alexis Beatrice Vandershoot

Alex and Peggy put their letters in the same envelope. Alex licked it.

"But you *swallowed* the tooth," said Peggy. "Do you think she'll still come?"

"Oh, yes," said Alex confidently. "That's how it works. Once I even wrote her when I hadn't lost a tooth and she came. But that was an emergency."

Alex made a little sign to put on the cookies: TOOTH FAIRY TREATS—FOR TOOTH FAIRIES WITH STRONG TEETH.

Alex opened the window a little bit, and then Peggy helped her clean up before they put on their pajamas.

"Feels a little like Christmas, doesn't it?" Peggy said.

Alex nodded. It was early for bed on a Friday, but that was okay. She and Peggy talked together awhile, and as she was going to sleep, she thought how nice it was to have Peggy in the sleeping bag next to her bed—something else for her list about why she liked having her own room.

"Alex!" The voice was a very loud whisper. "Are you awake? Did she come?"

"I don't know." Alex opened her sleepy eyes, scrunched over, and lifted up the covers so Peggy could crawl in next to her.

Alex reached under the pillow and pulled out an envelope. She felt around for another one. Nothing.

"Alexis Beatrice Vandershoot."

Peggy frowned. "Is there another one?"

"No."

"Do you think maybe there's a note inside for me?"

Alex popped open the seal. There was a single sheet of paper, with her name at the top. "What about under *your* pillow?"

Peggy dived for the floor and flipped over the pillow. "Yippee!" She got back in bed.

They cuddled up.

Alex stared at the envelope in Peggy's hand. It was from *her*, all right.

Peggy touched the swirl under her name. "I don't tell anyone my middle name."

"Me neither," said Alex. "She's good at middle names."

Dear Peggy,

What a nice surprise to hear from you. My correspondence list is not too terribly long, so of course I will write to you, though as Alexis may have mentioned I usually prefer to write when you've lost a tooth.

Glad to hear you're interested in magical creatures. Not many children these days are. It may intrigue you to know that I am interested in children— and not just for their teeth. What is school like? When do children stop being children?

Keep wiggling those teeth.

Your friend,
The Tooth Fairy

Peggy hugged her letter to her chest. "Let's read yours now."

Alex opened her letter.

Dear Alexis,

Thank you for the cookies. They tasted very human. And of course I must remember to brush when I get back to the castle. Perhaps I am being greedy, but I've taken the rest home with me for later.

Don't worry about the swallowed tooth. You would be amazed at some of the stories I hear about what happens to teeth.

About the moving request. You are right that moving often seems to be difficult, "a bad thing" as you put it. But often very good things can come about as a result—your friendship with Peggy, for example.

Alex and Peggy looked at each other.

So in answer to your question about never moving, I don't think that would be fair. Think of all the good things you might miss. But don't worry so much, or you'll miss out on the good things here and now. It certainly sounds to me as if your mother has a good head on her shoulders. You should listen to her and talk to her, too.

Love,
The T.F.

P.S. She can probably listen better if you talk to her when she's not doing six things at once.
P.P.S. Why do you think it is so much fun to write P.S. at the bottom of a letter?

Chapter 9

For weeks it had been the main topic of conversation for the kids in Mr. H's class.

Kelsey was going to be a tiger. Devin's sister had made him a great monster costume. Quinton planned to be a traffic light—"green and yellow circles on my shirt and red makeup all over my face." Cullen had a pumpkin costume, and Amanda wanted to be a cheerleader.

Mr. H even promised that if all the desks were cleaned out, he would wear a costume to school.

Alex listened as all the kids bragged about their costumes or how much candy they were going to get. Peggy couldn't quite make up her mind: a fairy godmother, a witch, or a troll? But although Alex didn't tell anyone, there was only one thing she could possibly be.

During math time Alex sketched possible costumes and wiggled her tooth, but not too much.

"If you're having a birthday party for eight kids," said Mr. H, "and you want three cookies apiece, how many cookies do you need in all?"

Alex doodled. She didn't bother putting up her hand. She always knew the answer. And he knew she always knew the answer. So she doodled and sometimes, if he really thought she wasn't paying attention, he might actually call on her.

She drew a figure with wings and a familiar face, then turned her attention back to her teeth. Most of the big ones were pretty much in. There was just that one incisor, the bottom one on the far left that was loose.

She shoved the tooth with her tongue, then used her finger.

The tooth moved easily, and it was starting to come loose on the back. Halloween was next Wednesday, six days away. She might make it. Then again she'd never tried to lose a tooth on a certain day before.

"Alex," called Mr. H, "are you listening?"

"Sure." She closed her notebook. "Could you please repeat the problem?"

"You go trick-or-treating to eleven houses. At each house you receive two pieces of candy. How do you—"

"Twenty-two pieces of candy!" Alex smiled.

Mr. H glared. "What arithmetic operation do you use to find the answer?"

"Multiplication," said Alex. "Or repeated addition."

Toby was playing with Prestin Lopes in the tree house out back. Penelope was doing her language arts on the couch. As far as Alex could tell, language arts didn't have anything to do with art. It was English for big kids.

"Penelope," she said, "don't you feel bad you're too big to go trick-or-treating?"

Penelope looked at her. "Do you feel bad you're too small to go to the Halloween dance?"

Alex shook her head. Dancing with boys or trick-or-treating? No contest. Alex went to her mom's worktable.

Mom was doing what she called concept work. It looked like doodling. A tire store wanted an invitation to a grand opening at its new location.

Alex stood next to her and started to neaten the piles of papers and pencils. "How about something like," thought Alex aloud, " 'We got *tired* of our old location and are *rolling up* our sleeves on Elm Street'?"

"Not bad." Mom's pencil moved fast, and in almost no time there was a picture of a little shop traveling on wheels, with a MOVING banner draped over the side. "I think we're going to have to up your rate."

Alex smiled as she stood near her mother's shoulder, watching. She took a deep breath.

144

"Mom," she said, "are you doing six things at once?"

Mom's head snapped around to Alex, and she set her pencil down. "No, sweetheart. I'm not doing anything at all."

Alex smiled inside. "I decided what I'd like to be for Halloween."

"Really?"

She had thought and thought about it, wanting to keep it a secret. But she had decided that she would need help, a lot of help. "I'm going to be the Tooth Fairy."

"Oh, really." Mom's eyebrows jumped. "And what do you think the Tooth Fairy wears?"

"Well," Alex spoke slowly, "the Tooth Fairy wears all manner of things."

"Overalls, maybe?"

"Sometimes," said Alex, trying not to smile at her mother's paint-stained outfit. Alex didn't know exactly why it was important to keep the story going. "But it would be a lot more fun to wear a fairy costume."

"I suppose you're right." Mom walked to the kitchen, got two mugs from the dishwasher, checked to make sure they were clean before making cocoa from packets.

"With wings," said Alex. "It has to have wings. So a good updraft will make flying more fun."

"You certainly have been reading up on the Tooth Fairy."

"Oh, yes. She's one of my favorite people."

Mom put her arm around Alex's shoulder. "And I'm sure you're one of her favorite people, too."

"So what about the costume?"

"Costumes really aren't my department." Mom smiled in a special way. "I mean I'm not very good at them. How about if we ask Laurel to help us out?"

Laurel was Peggy's mom and very good at sewing.

Alex made a face. Laurel was nice, but—"I'd really like you, and maybe Dad, to help me."

"Okay," said Mom, "as long as you promise not to make any more cookies for a while."

Over the next few days Alex worried about her costume and her tooth. Her tooth and her costume. She wiggled and she worried. She worried and she wiggled. But not too much—wiggling anyway. Alex was afraid the tooth was going to come out too early, and then she was afraid it wouldn't come out in time.

It just had to come out on Halloween Day.

Peggy had decided to be a witch. "I think it's more fun to dress up as something bad. Mom's making me this cool black cape, and I've got a hat and green makeup for my face . . . and even a *wart*."

Peggy didn't seem to notice that Alex wasn't talking about her outfit.

The night before Halloween—the "eve of Hallow's eve," Toby kept calling it—Mom and Dad helped her assemble and try on her costume. They were in her room, pinning and fixing and fussing with all the pieces. The costume was so cool! Alex twirled and curtsied and felt like she actually might float away. Somehow she stopped herself from jumping on the bed, but she couldn't stop herself from hugging Mom.

And that's when it happened.

Her tooth fell out.

And Alex started to cry.

"What's wrong?" asked Dad. "You like it when your teeth come out."

"I know." How could she explain? "But I wanted it to come out tomorrow."

"You can wait to put it under your pillow," said Mom. "I'm sure the Tooth Fairy will be flexible."

"Especially," said Dad, "since Alex *is* the Tooth Fairy."

She almost, but not quite, stopped crying. They wouldn't understand. She squeezed the offending tooth inside her hand. "I don't get to be in charge of *anything*. You guys say when it's time to move. We draw for chores. Mom picks what's for dinner. Toby and Penelope always get the TV remote. My friends won't write me . . . and . . . there's more, but I can't think of it right now."

"There's a lot of things we're not in charge of either," said Dad. "You just don't see them."

"But we are the chief worriers," said Mom. "You've got to trust us on that. We're always there and doing the worrying for you. Especially now. I don't think tears are going to help the Tooth Fairy costume. In fact, the Tooth Fairy has always struck me as a cheerful sort."

"She just wants people to think that."

"Maybe, maybe not," said Mom. "Why don't you write her a letter and ask her?"

Trick-or-treating was different here than in Texas.

It was colder, for one thing.

Even with a long-sleeved shirt on under her costume Alex shivered sometimes.

In Dallas, the goal was to get as much candy as possible. Kids carried huge bags, pillowcases even, and sometimes ran between the houses. Here the idea was more to have fun. Many of the parents wore costumes—even Dad put a patch over one eye—and there was sometimes a haunted porch to visit and always conversations at the door, especially since the Vandershoots were still new on the block.

"And who is this beautiful creature?" said the woman across the street.

Alex stood back and smiled. She moved slowly so as not to damage her delicate wings, but quickly and smoothly enough so that her sparkly cloth would poof out over the stiff petticoat and give the full effect of flying.

There was a ring of sparkles on her hair.

As she turned, the netting on the wings fluttered slightly. T.F. was lettered on each wing in gold, and as she moved, the lettering looked like some kind of magic words. Her basket had white construction-paper teeth and a little sign: WE CARE ABOUT TEETH. BETTER BRUSHING FOR BETTER LIVING.

Instead of regular shoes Alex wore her sister's old ballet slippers. And makeup, of course. Alex's lips were bright pink, and her eyes had some stuff on them that looked very Tooth Fairy-ish.

Peggy was wrong. It was more fun to dress up as something nice.

Alex curtsied to the woman. "I am the Tooth Fairy."

The woman laughed. "Can I tell you a secret?"

"Sure. I guess so." Alex leaned in.

"Do you come for grown-ups?" she whispered. "I'm getting false teeth next week, and I really would like to have something for these old teeth of mine."

Alex thought a second. "The Tooth Fairy is fair. Or else I wouldn't be called a fairy. I'll be happy to come visit you. But I need to tell you a secret about the Tooth Fairy."

"Yes?" whispered the woman.

"She likes to get mail. And not a scrawny post-card, either. A real letter."

"I'll keep that in mind," said the woman as she scooped up some chocolate.

Alex decided, as she skipped down the sidewalk, that she was going to pay the woman a visit and write her a little note.

Dear Tooth Fairy,

Mom said it was okay to write to you tonight. Even though I lost my tooth yesterday. It is my last incisor tooth. I am going to miss you. Maybe you will miss me, too.

Did you know that when you first wrote me I didn't even know how to spell Beatrice? There is a man down the street who is having puppies. Actually he is not having puppies. His dog is having puppies. Mom and Dad said we can pick one. I'm very excited, even if it is bribery. Toby is excited, even if it isn't a Saint Bernard.

I think it's fun to write P.S. on letters because then it's like they'll never end, like you're really there with the person—or fairy—going back for one last hug before you say good-bye.

Your friend forever,
Alexis Beatrice Vandershoot

Dear Alexis,

I have enjoyed your letters—as I enjoy you—very much. I will miss flying in to visit you this way, no maybes about it.

There's a right time for everything, and I guess it's time for you to go on to big-girl things, and it's time for me to once and for all get the castle tidied up.

But remember, if you ever need me, I'm always right there . . . closer than you think.

Love,
The Tooth Fairy

P.S. Can I borrow that wonderful costume of yours sometime?

Karen Ray is also the author of a novel for older readers, *To Cross a Line*. She and her family recently relocated from Texas to Switzerland.